DC SUPER HEROES

WONDER WOMAN

★ THE AMAZING AMAZON ★

ARES' UNDERWORLD ARMY

WRITTEN BY
LOUISE SIMONSON

ILLUSTRATED BY
LUCIANO VECCHIO

WONDER WOMAN CREATED BY
WILLIAM MOULTON MARSTON

STONE ARCH BOOKS
a capstone imprint

PUBLISHED BY STONE ARCH BOOKS IN 2018
A CAPSTONE IMPRINT
1710 ROE CREST DRIVE
NORTH MANKATO, MINNESOTA 56003
WWW.MYCAPSTONE.COM

CATALOGING-IN-PUBLICATION DATA IS AVAILABLE AT THE LIBRARY OF
CONGRESS WEBSITE.
ISBN: 978-1-4965-6531-0 (LIBRARY BINDING)
ISBN: 978-1-4965-6535-8 (PAPERBACK)
ISBN: 978-1-4965-6539-6 (EBOOK PDF)

SUMMARY: WITH THE HELP OF HADES, ARES UNLEASHES A
SKELETON ARMY ON GATEWAY CITY! WONDER WOMAN QUICKLY JUMPS
INTO ACTION, BUT AS THE CONFLICT GROWS SO DOES THE GOD OF
WAR'S POWER. CAN THE AMAZON WARRIOR SEND THE VILLAIN AND
HIS MINIONS BACK TO THE UNDERWORLD? OR WILL ARES AND HADES
PREVAIL WITH THEIR PERILOUS PARTNERSHIP?

EDITOR: CHRISTOPHER HARBO
DESIGNER: HILARY WACHOLZ

Printed and bound in Canada.
PA020

TABLE OF CONTENTS

With countries in chaos and the world at war, Earth faced its darkest hour. To answer its cry for help, the Amazons on the secret island of Themyscira held a trial to find their strongest and bravest champion. From that contest one warrior—Princess Diana—triumphed over all and boldly entered the world of mortals. Now her mission is to conquer villainy, defend justice, and restore peace across the globe.

She is . . .

WONDER WOMAN

★ THE AMAZING AMAZON ★

CHAPTER 1

THE CRACK IN THE WORLD

Wonder Woman soared above the skyscrapers of Gateway City. She wheeled out over the sparkling bay and then swept back toward midtown. She scanned the streets for trouble—for ways she could help. But for once the whole town seemed to be at peace.

Wonder Woman dipped low, skimming the treetops. She flew over Memorial Park with its neighborhood playgrounds and ball fields.

Then she heard angry shouts.

"I can't believe what you've done, Will!" a girl's voice yelled. "Why did your team tear up the park?"

"We didn't!" a boy's voice growled. "It wasn't us!"

What's up? Wonder Woman wondered. She stopped, hovering in the air high above a playground.

Below, rival softball players faced each other. Their team names—the Eastside Eagles and the Westend Warriors—were on their uniforms. A boy and a girl were shouting at each other, nose to nose. Their teams were backing them up. Wonder Woman thought a fight might break out at any moment.

The situation sounded pretty bad. But then Wonder Woman looked at the playground behind them. She realized what had happened there was far, far worse.

The playground equipment had been destroyed. Swing sets lay toppled onto the ground. The jungle gym was a twisted mess. The seesaws were splintered planks of wood.

A group of little kids were crying. Their moms and dads were gaping at the destruction. No one could believe their eyes.

Wonder Woman settled to the ground. Normally the appearance of the six-foot-tall Amazon Princess Diana would have caused everyone to stop and stare. But the kids were so focused on their argument they didn't notice her until she landed right beside them.

"What's going on?" Wonder Woman asked. "What happened here?"

The kids glanced at her in surprise. For an instant, Wonder Woman thought her arrival would put an end to the argument. But instead, it gave each side an audience.

"The Warriors messed up the playground," the girl shouted. She was the captain of the Eagles and appeared to have quite a temper. "Did you do this because we won the last five games, Will?"

"That was last year, Emma," Will, the captain of the Warriors, snarled. "This year, we're gonna cream you!"

"Like, how?" Emma growled. She pointed her bat at the nearby baseball park. The diamond was torn up. The bleachers were smashed. The bases were scattered. "You haven't left us a field to play on! I can see you Warriors doing *that*, but why destroy the playground too? We all played here when we were little. Our brothers and sisters and cousins play here now!"

Emma's teammates grumbled in agreement behind her.

"We didn't do it!" Will was nose to nose with Emma again. "We wouldn't! How could a bunch of kids make this mess, anyway?"

Wonder Woman thought Will had a point. This destruction was far beyond anything kids would be capable of. But that argument didn't convince Emma. She and her team just kept shouting. And Will and his team kept yelling back.

Wonder Woman was starting to get frustrated. Each side wanted to talk, but neither side wanted to listen. She unhooked her lasso. She knew one quick way to get the truth—if the kids would agree to the test.

* * *

Deep inside Earth, in a fiery underworld called Tartarus, two Greek gods faced each other across a chessboard.

Hades, the ruler of Tartarus, reached out and moved a pawn shaped like a skeleton. The pawn held a sword, just like the skeleton soldiers standing at attention behind him.

Hades' nephew Ares, the God of War, studied the chessboard through a small portal. The magical window linked Tartarus and Olympus, the realm of the gods where Ares lived. While the portal allowed Ares to reach in to play the game, it kept Hades from escaping his prison in Tartarus.

Ares reached through the portal and picked up a bishop. He moved it diagonally, knocking over Hades' warrior pawn.

"I've taken one of your pieces, Uncle," Ares said. "You're losing your touch."

"I have been trapped here far too long." Hades sighed. "But I will remain here as long as Queen Hippolyta holds the key."

Ares looked at him sharply. "And yet, rumors fly that you have found a crack in your realm. Some say your Skeleton Army can travel through it to the mortal realm of Earth."

HA·HA·HA·HA·HA! Hades let out a long, booming laugh.

"So *that* is why you agreed to this game, Nephew!" The Ruler of the Underworld shrugged. "The rumor is true. I sent a test squad through to Earth. And they returned with those." Hades pointed to a pile of chains and broken bits of wood tossed into a corner. "What could be more worthless?"

Ares studied the debris with interest. He noticed a piece of wood had PROPERTY OF GATEWAY CITY stamped on it. It looked like part of a large toy the mortals called a swing set.

Hades knew that Ares had been growing bored. Life on Olympus was far too peaceful for the God of War. Ares thrived on constant conflict and battle. And Hades' Skeleton Army fascinated him.

Hades pretended to study the chessboard. He waited for the ideas he had slyly planted to grow in Ares' mind.

Ares grinned. "Lend me your Skeleton Army, Uncle," he said eagerly. "I will bring you a greater reward than those chains and broken boards."

Hades frowned. "I don't know." He tried to sound unsure.

"Well then, let me win the Skeleton Army from you," Ares said, waving a hand above the chessboard. "If I beat you at this game of chess, you will let me command them!"

Hades shrugged. "If you win, then they will be yours—but only for as long as you win your battles on Earth. The moment you lose, they will return instantly to me!"

"Agreed," Ares said, staring at the chessboard and rubbing his hands gleefully.

Hades rose. "Then let me bring goblets to toast our upcoming battle of wits," he said. Then he walked away.

* * *

Wonder Woman stared at the bent metal and shattered wood in the Memorial Park playground. She needed to find out who or what had caused the destruction. She was pretty sure it wasn't any of the kids.

"Enough!" the hero said. Her voice was quiet, but commanding. The arguing stopped at once.

Wonder Woman unhooked her golden lasso and held it out for the kids to see. Will gaped. Emma gasped.

"This is my Lasso of Truth," Wonder Woman said.

"I know! It's magic!" Will said, suddenly excited. "Anybody who's tied up with it has to tell the truth!"

"So put it around him!" Emma said. "That will prove he's a liar!"

"I am not!" Will said. "Emma—"

"I suggest putting it around both of you," Wonder Woman said. "It's the fastest way—"

"—to prove what a liar Will is!" Emma exclaimed. "But I'll go first, just to show him I'm telling the truth."

"Fine. Prove it." Will folded his arms. "Then she can test me!"

Wonder Woman made a loop in the lasso. She slipped it over Emma's head and tightened it around her arms.

"Are you ready?" Wonder Woman asked.

Emma looked a little worried, but she nodded. "I'm ready."

"Did you or anyone on your team destroy this park?" Wonder Woman asked.

"No. We didn't," Emma said. She lifted the loop over her head and handed it to Will.

"Now you do it!" Emma demanded.

Will lowered the loop over his head and shoulders. Wonder Woman tightened it.

Before Wonder Woman could even ask a question, Will said, "I didn't do it. Nobody on my team did either. We wouldn't! And that's the truth."

Will pulled the loop over his head and handed it to Wonder Woman.

Emma frowned. She looked a little bit embarrassed. "But if you didn't do it . . . and we didn't do it, then who made this mess?"

"That's an excellent question," Wonder Woman said. She wound up her golden lasso and hooked it onto her waist. "That's what I need to find out."

CHAPTER 2

INVASION OF THE SKELETON ARMY

When Hades returned to Ares with the promised drinks, he noticed the chessboard gave off a faint, eerie glow. He had guessed right. He knew his nephew would do whatever it took to win.

Hades smiled as he handed Ares a golden goblet. "May the best god win!" he said.

"Oh, he will," Ares said smugly. "There is no doubt about that. No doubt at all."

From then on, no matter what move Hades made, Ares made a better one. Soon Ares had most of Hades' pieces jumbled in a pile before him.

Ares moved his queen and yelled, "Checkmate! I win!" He leaped to his feet, raising his arms in victory. "I now command your Skeleton Army. I cannot wait to join them in Gateway City."

Ares loved to watch mortals fight—after all, he drew his strength from their combat on Earth. The greater the conflict, the stronger, the bigger, and the more powerful he became. It made him laugh just to think about it.

Hades frowned, pretending to look worried. "You know Wonder Woman is in Gateway City, Nephew," he said. "She's sure to join the battle!"

Ares grinned. "I'm counting on it, Uncle. I love forcing Wonder Woman to fight! Though she's made for war, her ultimate goal is peace. Such a waste, but I will enjoy trying to change her mind!"

Ares rose. "And now, Uncle, send my new army through the crack in your realm. I will meet them in Memorial Park!"

Hades shrugged. "Go then, Ares. Use my army." He waved a careless hand and his skeleton warriors began to march toward a distant crack in the wall. "Have fun!"

"Believe me, Uncle! I will," Ares said.

Hades smiled as he closed the portal and Ares faded from view. "So young. So confident. But not so sure of himself against me," he murmured. "Ares felt he had to cheat to make sure he won. And he played right into my hands."

Hades smiled as he watched his warriors disappear through the distant passage to Earth. "Wonder Woman's mother, Hippolyta, holds the key to my prison. And I want that key. So Ares will face Diana—nose to nose. And thus he will learn he has stumbled right into my trap."

* * *

"OH NO! LOOK!" Wonder Woman and the teams whirled at a woman's cry of dismay and wails from the little kids.

What is going on? the hero thought.

Then they watched in horror as a wave of armored, sword-wielding skeletons poured out of thin air. They tumbled like a river of bones through the Memorial Park playground and surged toward the wrecked baseball fields beyond.

The parents picked up the little kids. They backed away as skeletons ran past and swiped their swords at fences, trees, and playground equipment.

Whatever is happening, it has to stop! Wonder Woman thought. She leaped forward and smashed into a group of skeletons.

POW!

The monsters were much stronger than they looked and, at first, they almost overwhelmed the Amazon warrior. But then Wonder Woman swung her fist.

WHAKK!

A skeleton's skull went flying. The warrior collapsed into a pile of bones.

So they aren't invulnerable, after all, the hero thought. *Wherever they came from, they can be stopped.*

Wonder Woman fought with all her might, and skull after skull toppled from bony shoulders. But, strong as she was, Diana was just one person. And no matter how many monsters collapsed, others poured through the invisible hole to take their place.

While Wonder Woman stopped as many as she could reach, others dashed past her into the park. To her horror, some even moved toward the kids.

But the softball teams had been watching Wonder Woman fight. Will had seen how she defeated the monsters.

"We aren't helpless!" he said. He swung his bat. **WHAKK!** An attacking skeleton crumbled into a pile of dust.

"Good hit," Emma called to Will. Then she jumped into action, swinging her bat too! The rest of the players followed.

WHAK! WHAK! WHAM! One by one, the monsters crumpled into piles of bones.

Seeing the kids were safe, Wonder Woman leaped into the air and looked around. Almost all of the skeletons that had gotten past her were heading into the rest of the park and rushing toward the city streets. A continuous stream of skeletons appeared out of nowhere and rushed after them.

"The playground is just their gateway. We know where they're coming from. Now I have to find out where they're going!" Wonder Woman called down to the kids. "Will you be all right?"

"We'll be fine," Will said. "Most of those monsters aren't interested in us anyway."

Emma nodded fiercely. "And if they change their minds, we have our bats. But what are they doing here?"

"I don't know," Wonder Woman said grimly. "But I need to find out."

She herded the children and adults into a nearby equipment shed. It was constructed of brick and had thick metal bars on the window.

"Stay there," she said. "Keep the door closed. Keep watch. Don't come out till it's safe. And somebody use a cell phone to call the police."

Will fumbled in his pocket and pulled out his cell phone. "Good idea," he said. "I'll call the cops right away!"

Emma and the other kids raised their bats like clubs. "And we're ready to protect the others if necessary!" Emma looked like she hoped it would be necessary. "Just don't let those monsters get out into the city!"

That's what I'm worried about, Wonder Woman thought. *What if there are too many of them? What if I can't stop them?*

Wonder Woman flew above the Skeleton Army as it rushed through the park and over the playing fields. The monsters used their swords to hack at benches, statues, and trees.

WHAK! SLASH! CRACK!

Joggers, dog-walkers, and couples holding hands ran screaming.

Several skeletons swerved after a woman pushing a stroller and holding the hand of a curly-haired toddler. She tried to run, but the monsters were almost upon her.

Wonder Woman flew down and scooped the mother, toddler, and baby stroller up into her arms. She needed to take them somewhere safe.

Looking around, the hero spotted a small snack bar building beside a shallow lake in the distance. She carried the woman and her children to it and landed in the courtyard.

People seated at tables looked up in surprise. "It's Wonder Woman!" Several people stood. Almost everyone pulled out cameras and cell phones to take pictures.

"There's a park emergency," Wonder Woman said in a clear, calm voice. "Please get inside the snack bar and lock the doors. Don't come out until the police tell you it's safe to do so."

The people looked confused.

"There are monsters!" the rescued mother said in a shaky voice. "I saw them! Wonder Woman saved me. Please, we all have to do what she says."

The snack bar manager held the door open and waved everyone inside. The rescued mother carried her children toward the door. The other people followed slowly, until one skeleton, then another appeared on a path. Then there was a mad rush into the building.

Wonder Woman flew at the skeletons. She slammed one with her fist and high kicked the other. The two monsters crumbled into bones. Looking back, Diana saw the restaurant manager slam the door shut and lock it firmly.

* * *

We're lucky it's early afternoon and most people are still at work, Wonder Woman thought as she flew into the air. *I'll have to double back and see where the skeletons are heading. They obviously have a goal, almost like they're following someone's orders.*

Wonder Woman flew high enough to see the skeletons moving like army ants. They swept past a small boat pond toward a wide tree-lined meadow. Next came a cross street. The Memorial Park Zoo was just beyond.

What will happen when the skeletons reach the zoo? Wonder Woman worried. *Will they free the lions, tigers, bears, and elephants? Will the animals pour into the city beyond? That will just add more danger.*

WHOOP! WHOOP! WHOOP!

Wonder Woman heard the wail of sirens and saw the flash of red, white, and blue lights. Will had gotten through to the police! The cops were coming!

Patrol cars zoomed up the Memorial Park roadways. The cars screeched to a halt, and police officers leaped from the doors.

For an instant, the officers stood gaping as they faced their monstrous enemies. Wonder Woman knew Will had told the cops about the skeletons, but seeing them was obviously a shock. The police looked like they couldn't quite believe their eyes.

The skeletons stopped their advance as well. They seemed equally surprised by the screaming sirens and flashing lights.

The cops were the first to pull themselves together. They stepped forward bravely, ready to protect their city against the sword-wielding monsters.

The skeletons rushed at the officers. But before they could reach the cops, Wonder Woman dropped from the sky. She landed between both sides just as they were about to clash.

CHAPTER 3

THE WAR OF BONES

Ares suddenly appeared on the top of the arched stone gateway that led into the Memorial Park Zoo. He looked around.

The zoo was small. It was a quiet, peaceful afternoon.

In the center of the zoo's courtyard sat a pond. Seals and sea lions splashed in the water and climbed onto rocks. Tourists and mothers with children watched as a zookeeper fed fish to a performing seal.

Ares shrugged and turned his attention elsewhere.

Walkways led to buildings that housed lions, tigers, bears, and elephants. There was even a reptile house.

Ares smiled.

Given time, and my influence, these animals have interesting possibilities, Ares thought. *But for now, this place is too quiet! Too boring! Where is the Skeleton Army I was promised?*

Suddenly men, women, and children ran out of the park. They dashed through the gateway he stood on, into the zoo, and out its exit gates to reach the city beyond.

Finally! Ares thought. He leaped into the air, eager with anticipation. He squinted through the trees, trying to see what surely must be below.

Ares could hear the sounds of the conflict now. The shouts of men. The clash of swords. The scream of sirens.

And then the army of skeletons—his army—swarmed into view!

He flew higher still. *Where is the battle?* he wondered.

Police cars had pulled up near a field, lights flashing. The cops were trying to cut off the skeleton soldiers.

"There!" Ares said to himself as Wonder Woman landed. For an instant, she stood against the swarm, trying to protect the city's protectors.

"Those men and women are warriors, Diana," Ares murmured. "They won't thank you for shielding them. Not that you have a chance of doing so."

As the first wave of skeletons swept over Wonder Woman, she went down beneath the onslaught. For an instant, Ares thought she might even have been crushed beneath their endless numbers.

Then skeleton bodies went flying. The Amazon warrior leaped into the air, kicking out and spinning.

WHAK! WHAK! WHAK!

Wonder Woman's foot connected with skeleton skulls, and their bodies collapsed into dust around her.

But Wonder Woman couldn't stop them all alone. The monsters swarmed past her, swords swinging, to clash with the police.

"Use your nightsticks," the hero called out to the cops. "These skeletons are strong and mindless, but they're not invulnerable."

Officers pulled out their clubs and started swinging wildly.

CRACK! WHAK! WHAM!

Skeleton after skeleton collapsed into a heap of bones.

But more skeletons grabbed Wonder Woman with magically strong arms and pulled her under a second wave of clawing monsters. Ares grinned as she disappeared. *Is this how the life of Diana, Amazon Princess of Themyscira, will end?* he wondered.

Then Wonder Woman fought her way into the air for a second time. More skulls flew off. More skeleton warriors crumbled around her. But most of the army swept past.

Proudly, Ares watched them come to him. They sought their commander—Ares, God of War—who would lead them to victory!

What an army they will make! he thought.
*Under my command, this endless horde of
skeletons will take control of Gateway City.
Then they'll sweep across the continent, causing
conflict and destruction wherever they appear.
And my power—my strength, my glory—will
grow with every battle.*

HA! HA! HA!

Ares laughed with delight. In seconds, he
knew Diana would realize her actions were
completely useless. He looked forward to
watching her despair.

But Wonder Woman broke free of the
skeleton warriors for a third time and soared
into the air once more. Ares saw her face
as she watched the monsters, his monsters,
rushing headlong toward the zoo. He could
tell their numbers had her puzzled. She didn't
have a clue how to stop them!

Ares' army of bones poured through the stone gate. Then, in the courtyard below, they stopped and stared up at him with empty eye sockets. They had arrived as Hades had promised. They awaited orders from their commander.

"Smash the animal cages!" Ares ordered. "Free the beasts to roam and destroy!"

Skeletons splashed into the seal pond. They picked up stones and tossed them to make a ramp so the seals and sea lions could escape.

RIPP!

The skeletons tore the doors off the building that housed the reptiles.

CRASH!

They smashed the fences that held the lions, tigers, bears, and elephants.

The frightened animals burst from their cages. Bears growled. Lions roared. Elephants trumpeted. An alligator slithered between their feet, jaws snapping.

Wonder Woman left the battle between the cops and skeletons. She flew above Ares' head and landed in the zoo's courtyard.

Ares grinned. *Wonder Woman is so distracted by the chaos, she hasn't even noticed me,* he thought. *She's still trying to get ahead of my army before they rush into the city.*

The skeleton warriors attacked Wonder Woman, and she fought them bravely. Ares watched as skulls flew off shoulders and bones crumbled to dust around her.

Diana had learned to deal with these mindless creatures one on one. But their numbers still confounded her. Trying to stop his army was like trying to hold back a flood.

Below Ares, a child screamed. A lion stalked a boy clinging to his little sister.

In a flash, Wonder Woman flew into the air. As the lion leaped, she snatched up the children.

"You're safe now," she said and dropped them gently onto the roof of the Elephant House. "Stay here where none of the animals can reach you! Someone will come for you when the coast is clear."

On the ground behind her, a tiger snarled a challenge to the angry lion. Ares grinned. It would be amusing to watch these big cats battle each other.

But before that clash could begin, Wonder Woman dove toward them. She snatched up the lion by his mane. Ares realized she planned to discourage the fight by separating the animals.

Then Ares had a better idea. *Let's see how our Amazon Princess reacts to a skeleton lion,* he thought.

The villain waved his hand and the lion began to glow. Then suddenly, it turned into a skeleton in Wonder Woman's hands.

For an instant Wonder Woman hesitated with shock. And in that moment, the skeleton lion twisted and raked her arm with its claws.

The Amazon warrior was invulnerable to most things, but not always to magic. The claws scratched, but the cuts healed instantly.

"Magical attacks, magical wounds," she murmured.

Wonder Woman dropped the lion skeleton into a damaged cage and bent the metal bars back into place.

"You stay there till I get this sorted out!" the hero said.

"So easily distracted." Ares smirked. It was clear Diana now knew that magic was involved. She would try to keep even these wild animals safe, hoping to find a way to restore them.

Still foolishly trying to protect everyone, even lions, alligators, and bears, he thought. *Still trying to bring peace to the world. What a heroic idiot!*

Ares loved it. He wanted more!

The villain waved an arm and an elephant, a bear, and a tiger became skeletons as well. Their huge, sharp teeth gleamed in their massive skulls. Then they leaped on Wonder Woman, a tangle of bones, teeth, and claws.

That should keep the young princess busy while I lead my army into the city, Ares thought. He knew it was time to move on, but still he stopped to watch her fight. He was curious to see what she'd do next.

One by one, Wonder Woman separated her animal attackers. She was careful not to harm them, even though their scratches and bites scored her skin. She carried the skeleton animals to separate cages, locked them in, and repaired the fencing.

Ares knew he *should* get going. His army was waiting. But the villain was distracted now. Pushing Diana was fun. Except—

Suddenly Ares realized: *She's so intent on ending these battles, she hasn't figured out I'm behind them! And where's the fun in that?*

Ares was itching to join the fight.

The God of War settled onto the stone arch and pointed. Skeleton warriors surged toward Wonder Woman. Ares wanted her distracted while he decided what to do next.

Skeletons were the theme of this great conflict—and he was a master of transformation. He could *become* a skeleton too. But a skeleton warrior was too ordinary. Ares wanted something unique.

An animal shape might be fun, he thought. *But nothing ordinary. Something different. Something monstrous!*

"Cerberus!" Ares said. With the wave of his hand, the giant, three-headed dog was standing atop the arch.

"Not fierce enough," Ares muttered. "What else?" He thought of all the legendary monsters that lived in glorious Olympus. *Griffin. Harpy. Hydra. Manticore.*

"Chimera!" the God of War shouted.

Immediately, Ares changed into a massive monster with the head and body of a lion, the pointed horns of a goat, and a long, thick snake for a tail.

Fierce! Ares thought. He opened his mouth and roared.

RHARRRGH!

A blast of both noise and flame erupted from his jaws. *I can breathe fire! Good!*

"But Diana can fly," Ares muttered. "And a Chimera can't. Unless . . . "

"Am I a god or what?" Ares growled. "I'll give my Chimera body the batlike wings of a dragon. Who is there to stop me?"

And suddenly, the Chimera had wings. "But there's still the skeleton theme," Ares murmured. "I wonder . . . "

Ares waved a paw and his winged Chimera shed its flesh. It stood, massive and frightening, a gigantic creature of gleaming bones. Even its batlike wings were thin rods of bone.

Ares flapped his wings and leaped skyward. "It probably wouldn't fly in reality," he muttered. "But altering reality *is* a hobby of mine."

The villain circled the field where skeleton warriors and police officers clashed. As the conflict raged below, he soaked up its fury. His Chimera skeleton grew even larger.

Ares roared, and his flaming breath burned brighter. This new monstrous body delighted him. And, huge as it was, it would continue to grow—larger and stronger—as the conflict raged on.

Now it was Diana's turn.

There she is! he thought. *Battling her skeleton enemies—warriors and animals, together. Still trying to protect the animals that are—most ungratefully—trying to bite and scratch her. She's such a fool. It is just too funny.*

The Chimera dropped to the ground with a **THUD**. Skeleton warriors crunched beneath its massive foot bones as it settled behind Wonder Woman. It folded its huge bony wings—and bellowed.

RHAHHHHH!

Flames leaped from the monster's mouth and swept over Wonder Woman.

CHAPTER 4

THE BATTLE OF TEETH AND CLAWS

Invulnerability kept Wonder Woman's skin from blistering, but she still felt pain from the magical flames. She whirled to face this new opponent. Her eyes widened at the sight of the huge skeletal monster.

A Chimera! Wonder Woman thought. *Or the skeleton of one!*

Its massive skull was definitely that of a lion. Pointed goat's horns stood out like spears from its bony brow. And its skeletal tail had a snake's skull at its tip.

What is it doing here? she wondered. *A Chimera isn't a creature of Earth, like the lions and bears in the zoo. It's a magical being from Olympus.*

The monster sprang at Wonder Woman with its jaws open wide. ***SNAPPT!***

The hero leaped into the sky, barely avoiding its massive teeth.

The Chimera unfurled its wings and soared into the air after her.

Wonder Woman was startled. *The Chimera of legend can't fly,* she thought. *If this isn't a Chimera—or not one exactly—what is it? Could it be an illusion?*

The Chimera swiped at her with catlike claws. A massive talon caught her arm, leaving a gash that healed slower than those made by the earthly animals.

It's definitely not an illusion, Wonder Woman thought.

The hero pushed herself higher. It was clear this creature was a solid being. And one filled with godlike magic, many times that of the other skeleton animals. She could feel it throbbing in the gash on her arm.

So, am I facing a magical creature? she wondered. *Or an Olympian god who has changed himself into that monstrous shape?*

If it is a god transformed—and, from the power it projects, I think it must be—I'll have to be careful, the Amazon realized. *I need to lead it out over the ocean, away from the people. I can't let it set fire to Gateway City.*

Wonder Woman whirled and flew away from the park. She soared out over the bay, speeding over sailboats, barges, and even a ferry.

The Chimera raced after the Amazon warrior. She zigzagged away from it, trying to escape its flames. The famous Gateway Bridge loomed just ahead, filled with bumper-to-bumper cars, as usual.

The Amazon Princess was fast, but the creature was gaining on her.

SNAP!

Wonder Woman could almost feel its teeth nipping at her heels. She was already flying at top speed. She couldn't keep it up forever.

The Chimera roared again.

RAHRRR!

Flames licked at Wonder Woman's legs. She needed a way to slow the monster down or even stop it.

Below, the bay—cold and dark—seemed to call to her. And she thought, *Why not?*

SPLASH! Wonder Woman dove into the water. Beneath the waves, the world felt icy. After the Chimera's constant noise it felt strangely peaceful. Suddenly, she could think. As she began putting the pieces of the puzzle together, she swam deeper.

First the Skeleton Army appeared out of nowhere. Where did it come from? she asked herself. *Hades, the Ruler of the Underworld, has an undead army, but he's trapped in Tartarus. So, if this is Hades' army, and he isn't commanding it, then who is?*

SPLASH!

The gigantic skeletal shape slammed into the water behind Wonder Woman. **CHOMP!** Massive teeth snapped at her, missing her by inches. Horns swerved to skewer her. She swam for the surface and launched herself into the air once more.

The monster flapped its bony wings and followed. It opened its mouth to scream, to breathe fire. What emerged was a gurgling **COUGH** and a puff of damp smoke.

It worked! Wonder Woman thought.

Water had quenched the creature's flames. And it seemed slower now. She knew it must be getting tired, but then, so was she.

Wonder Woman needed to find out who she was dealing with to have any hope of saving Gateway City. She glanced back at the monster chasing her.

"If only you could talk!" she muttered.

Why not? the hero thought. *Just because it hasn't said anything, doesn't mean it can't. Gods are proud and known to brag. Can I taunt him into speaking? Maybe, but first I need to end this chase.*

The Amazon warrior whirled suddenly and flew under the monster. As it rushed over her, she grabbed one of its bony paws, flew upward, and let go. She flipped the skeleton monster upside down!

For a moment the creature hung in midair. Its face registered shock—near panic—as it began to fall backward toward the waves. Then it twisted its body and hovered upright, wings spread.

"Enough of this ridiculous fight," Wonder Woman said, trying to make her voice drip with scorn. "A Chimera? Really? Made out of bones? What? You needed to keep the silly skeleton theme going a bit longer?"

Infuriated, the Chimera flapped its wings and charged her. It tried to gore her with its long, pointed horns. Wonder Woman dodged, but one horn grazed her arm.

HSSSST! The skull at the end of the monster's tail snapped as it flew past.

"You've finally decided to stop running," the creature said. "Good. I found your cowardice disappointing."

Good, he's talking, Wonder Woman thought. *And . . . it looks like he's grown even larger! Now to find out who he is and what he wants.*

"I *was* running from you," she agreed. "Surely you understand why. And can you guess why I've now stopped?"

"Of course I knew what you were doing." The Chimera sounded disgusted as it glanced down at the bay. "You were trying to lure me away from the city to protect those useless mortals. And you've stopped now because you think they're safe. But you're wrong."

The Chimera dropped toward the Gateway Bridge, rumbling like a train engine. Sparks leaped from its throat as it tried to work up to a mighty flaming bellow.

Wonder Woman looked at the dense traffic on the bridge and the ferry below it. *The Chimera's beginning to recover from its dunking,* she thought. *I can't let it set fire to anything!*

The Amazon Princess sped after the creature. Grabbing it by its serpent tail, she spun, whirling around and around. Then she let go, hurling the monstrous body farther out to sea.

The Chimera spread its wings, stopping itself in midair. It whirled and flew at the Amazon warrior, jaws wide. "You, who preach peace, are always so eager to leap into battle," it snarled.

It is definitely larger now, Wonder Woman thought. *Is its rapid growth a clue to its true identity? That's it!*

The Amazon warrior zipped skyward, avoiding the creature's searing breath as it screamed past her.

The monster whirled to face her. "You are glorious when you do what you do best, Diana," it said. "Don't waste your talent for war on an absurd quest for peace!"

Instead of rushing her again, the Chimera dove toward the water. That surprised her. *What was it thinking?* she wondered.

Then Wonder Woman realized a tour boat crammed with sightseers was floating right below them. She dove after the monster and threw herself between it and the tourists.

WHUMPH!

The Chimera roared fire, but the Amazon Princess hovered there. She shielded the terrified boaters with her own body.

"Sometimes you *have* to fight *for* what's right—and *against* what's wrong!" Wonder Woman said as the monster raced toward her. "And attacking these mortals is definitely wrong!"

The monster slammed into the hero. *HSSSSST!* Its snake tail whipped forward with lightning speed and—*THUNK*—sharp fangs sunk into her shoulder.

Wonder Woman slumped in midair. She appeared to grow weak as the creature's venom spread through her body.

SHRIEEEK! With a triumphant cry, the monster threw its bony claws around the Amazon Princess.

Getting this close to the Chimera had been dangerous, but Wonder Woman knew her ploy was the quickest way to end this mad game. She believed her Amazon powers would make her invulnerable to the snake's poison. But, even if it didn't, she couldn't let the Chimera continue its attack.

Clinging to Wonder Woman fiercely, the monster howled, "Foolish Amazon! Your quest for peace has earned you nothing but eternal rest!"

"Don't be so sure of that—Ares!" the Amazon Princess said. She wrenched her lasso from its clasp and threw it over the Chimera's massive head. "It is Ares, isn't it?"

Reacting to the golden lasso's power to force anyone bound by it to tell the truth, the skeletal Chimera began to fade. Slowly, Ares' true godly form began to appear.

"What do you want?" Wonder Woman demanded. "Why did you come to Earth? Why are you commanding Hades' army?"

But as Ares opened his fading Chimera jaws to speak, Gateway City suddenly disappeared. Still clutching Wonder Woman in his massive claws, the monster was pulled headlong into a realm of fire.

Ares, still not completely himself, dropped Wonder Woman. She pulled her lasso from around his torso and turned to face the Ruler of the Underworld.

Hades smiled. "Welcome to Tartarus, Princess Diana!"

CHAPTER 5

THE REAL VILLAIN

Wonder Woman watched amazed as, one by one, the skeleton warriors appeared in the huge, fire-rimmed cavern. They stood at attention in row after row behind Hades. Soon the whole undead army had returned.

The God of the Underworld turned to Ares. "As you see, Nephew, because you lost your battle, I have recalled my army. Still, you promised me a thing of value if you acted as their commander. Indeed, your gift of Wonder Woman is priceless."

"Gift?" Ares said.

Wonder Woman sighed. At least the invasion of skeleton soldiers had ended. "And what about the zoo animals?" she asked.

"Restored to their true forms," Ares grumbled. "The second I was pulled from the mortal realm my magic faded. But some are still running free."

Wonder Woman knew that wasn't great, but catching a few animals roaming the park would be easier than fighting an army. Still she had a few more questions.

"I can see that you wanted me, Hades. But why did you send Ares to collect me?" she asked. "Is he your messenger boy?"

Hades laughed. "I didn't send him. He insisted—even cheated at a game of chess to win the honor."

"I didn't," Ares sputtered angrily. "Or not exactly. He told me—! I was duped into it!" he shrieked.

Hades chuckled. "Well, I did think he would be more likely than my army to defeat you. And he exceeded my expectations when he became a skeleton himself."

"You *wanted* me to mimic your warriors?" Ares growled.

"I thought you might not be able to resist the temptation." A smile spread across Hades' face. "The magic that imprisons me would never have let you in if it believed you to be alive. But as a skeleton—and with Diana hidden in your bony clutches? It was almost too easy to trap you both!"

"So you wanted me here, Hades. Why?" Wonder Woman asked.

Hades shrugged. "I thought it would be obvious. I'll trade you for the key to Tartarus, which Hippolyta, your mother, holds. I'll use it to escape this prison!"

Wonder Woman's mind raced. *So Hades wants Hippolyta to choose,* she thought. *Lose her beloved daughter or loose Hades on the world. I can't let my mother face that decision.*

Somehow the Skeleton Army traveled from here to Earth, she reasoned. *Maybe I can take the same route home—if I can learn how they did it. And the best way to find that out is to keep these two gods bragging about their cleverness.*

"My mother will never give you the key, Hades. No matter what you threaten to do to me," Wonder Woman said.

The hero turned to Ares. "And you'll be trapped here with your uncle forever."

"I'm not trapped!" Ares snarled. He pointed into the distance. "There is a crack in Tartarus' wall—a dimensional portal that opens into Memorial Park. I am not my scheming uncle, so I am free to leave through that. From Gateway City, it is an easy teleport to my home on Olympus!"

That was all Wonder Woman needed to know. Without another word, she leaped into the air. She soared through heat and flames, racing in the direction Ares had pointed.

"Idiot nephew, don't let her escape!" Hades shouted. "After her!"

Even as Ares leaped into the air, his body morphed into a winged Chimera once more. This time he didn't become a skeleton and he moved as fast as Wonder Woman—maybe even faster. She had a head start, but he had a chance of catching her.

WHUMPH! WHUMPH! WHUMPH!

Flapping his wings and roaring flames,
Ares gave chase.

Hades flew behind them, amused, once
again, by how blindly Ares did his bidding.
The skeleton soldiers raced after them, swords
waving and armor clattering. But they soon
fell behind.

Wonder Woman dodged stalactites and
stalagmites. She soared over pits of bubbling
lava. Behind her, she heard the flapping of
massive wings. Ares was gaining on her.

Wonder Woman squinted through smoke
and flames, trying to spot the crack that
opened from this dimension into her own.

There! the hero thought, spotting a gleam
of blue in the wall. *That has to be the sky of
Earth!*

Putting on a final burst of speed, Wonder Woman raced toward the crack. Then she dove through it into Memorial Park.

But Ares was right behind her. And Hades and the skeletons were on his heels.

"Hades, you will never get the key!" Wonder Woman shouted. She jerked her lasso from its catch and touched the crack with it.

"By my lasso's magic, the true spell that seals off the Realm of the Dead from the Land of the Living is restored," she said, "You are trapped in Tartarus forever, Hades. And now, Ares, you are trapped there with him!"

"Noooo!" Ares shouted, rushing full steam for the crack. To his horror, it was beginning to close. The villain pumped his Chimera's wings even harder, trying desperately to make it through in time.

BA·BOOM! With a flash of energy, the crack slammed shut. The Chimera, unable to stop, crashed into a solid wall. **WHAM!**

After a moment, Ares picked himself up and returned to his godly form. In a rage, he tried to teleport out of Tartarus. Nothing happened.

"It won't work," Hades said, landing behind him. "Believe me, I've tried! The crack is sealed and the gates of Tartarus remain closed. But in a way I still win, for at least I now have company."

"You planned this?" Ares snarled.

Hades shrugged. "I foresaw it as one possible outcome. You cheated to win, Nephew. See where it got you? Still, I have no doubt that eventually you'll find a way to escape. In the meantime, how about a nice *honest* game of chess?"

* * *

In Memorial Park, the baseball players watched in amazement as Wonder Woman suddenly appeared out of nowhere. She flipped in midair, snatched up her lasso, and held it against—

"What is that?" Emma said. When she looked closer, she seemed to see a crack in the air. It glowed like fire.

Will stood beside her. "I don't know. I've never seen anything like it," he said.

Wonder Woman said something fast, and the glowing crack was suddenly gone.

The hero turned to the kids. She saw that the rival teams were working together to pick up the rubble.

"What happened here?" she asked.

"Skeletons were pouring out of the—the crack, or whatever that was," Emma said.

"And then suddenly they all just disappeared. Even the bones and skulls and dust!" Will continued. "How did you stop it?"

Wonder Woman smiled at them and began to help with the cleanup. "I found the villain who caused the trouble," she said. "He won't be able to send the Skeleton Army here again."

Wonder Woman grabbed the toppled swing set, flew into the air, and then set it down upright.

"Thanks," Will said. He and Emma picked up the tangled chains and seats that used to hang from swing set.

"My team is cleaning things up faster than your team," Emma said.

"They are not!" Will said. "Our pile of junk is higher than yours!"

Wonder Woman straightened some of the bars on the jungle gym. At least that piece of equipment might be salvaged.

GROWWWWR!

A loud growl sounded nearby. Everyone startled.

"Can you manage the cleanup alone—at least for a while?" Wonder Woman asked. "There's a bear I have to put back in a cage. And maybe an elephant."

"A bear? Uh, sure. We'll be fine!" Emma said, looking worried.

"We'll be better *without* wild animals around, anyway," Will said.

Wonder Woman flew into the air. "It's good to see you working together," she said.

"We're not, like, *friends* just because this happened," Emma said.

"Yeah!" Will said. "The rivalry's still on! It's just that the little kids need a safe place to play."

"And . . . we remember being kids here. Playing together. How much fun it was," Emma said wistfully.

Wonder Woman smiled. "Nobody said you had to be friends. But you've found a reason to work together. And that's a very good start."

ARES

BASE:
Mount Olympus

SPECIES:
Olympian God

OCCUPATION:
God of War

HEIGHT:
6 feet 11 inches

WEIGHT:
495 pounds

EYES:
Blue

HAIR:
Blond

POWERS/ABILITIES:
Immortality, unmatched strength, shape-shifting, teleportation, and indestructible armor. He is also a skilled military leader and strategist.

BIOGRAPHY:

Although his father is Zeus, the King of the Gods, Ares has never fit in on Mount Olympus. From an early age, he vowed to conquer Earth and overtake the human race. As the God of War, he thrives on conflict and enjoys manipulating humans into fighting with one another. With the powers of teleportation, shape-shifting, and incredible strength, Ares excels at causing chaos and destruction across the globe. Thankfully, Earth has Wonder Woman on its side, born to stop Ares' threats of treachery and death.

- One trait Ares prizes the most is that the larger a conflict grows, the more his powers increase. The villain relishes this trait so much he once had a weapon built for him that could mimic it. The Annihilator was a self-propelled battlesuit that fed on human rage.

- The God of War has several children, each with their own evil powers. Phobos, the God of Fear, can turn any nightmare into a reality. Deimos, the God of Terror, has a beard of snakes with panic-inducing venom. And Eris, the Goddess of Strife, can fill the hearts of her victims with hatred with just a bite of her Golden Apples of Discord.

- Ares might be Zeus' son, but the Amazon Princess counters him with powers she received from several goddesses. Demeter granted Wonder Woman strength and Aphrodite gave her beauty and a loving heart. In addition, Athena allowed her to talk to animals and Hermes granted her speed and flight. With these superpowers, Wonder Woman is Ares' most difficult foe.

BIOGRAPHIES

Louise Simonson enjoys writing about monsters, science fiction, fantasy characters, and super heroes. She has authored the award-winning Power Pack series, several best-selling X-Men titles, the Web of Spider-Man series for Marvel Comics, and the Superman: Man of Steel series for DC Comics. She has also written many books for kids. Louise is married to comic artist and writer Walter Simonson and lives in the suburbs of New York City.

Luciano Vecchio was born in 1982 and is based in Buenos Aires, Argentina. As a freelance artist for many projects at Marvel and DC Comics, his work has been seen in print and online around the world. He has illustrated many DC Super Heroes books for Capstone, and some of his recent comic work includes *Beware the Batman*, *Green Lantern: The Animated Series*, *Young Justice*, *Ultimate Spider-Man*, and his creator owned web-comic, *Sereno*.

GLOSSARY

commander (kuh-MAND-ur)—a person who leads an army

confound (kuhn-FOUND)—causing surprise or confusion

dupe (DOOP)—to trick

gore (GOR)—to pierce with horns

invulnerable (in-VUHL-nur-uh-buhl)—unable to be harmed

morph (MORF)—to change shape

mortal (MOR-tuhl)—human, referring to a being who will eventually die

portal (POR-tuhl)—a doorway, gate, or other entrance

rivalry (RYE-val-ree)—a fierce feeling of competition between two teams

stalactites (stuh-LAK-tites)—growths that hang from the ceiling of a cave and were formed by dripping water

stalagmites (stuh-LAG-mites)—growths that stand on the floor of a cave and were formed by drips of water from above

venom (VEN-uhm)—a poisonous liquid produced by some animals

DISCUSSION QUESTIONS

1. Hades tricks Ares into using his skeleton soldiers to attack Gateway City and capture Wonder Woman. Why does he do this? Why didn't he just lend his army to Ares outright? Discuss.

2. Wonder Woman uses her Lasso of Truth to prove that neither Emma's nor Will's teams destroyed the playground. Have you ever been in a situation where a Lasso of Truth would have helped solve a problem? Describe what happened and explain how the lasso would have helped.

3. Ares not only uses skeleton soldiers, but he also turns the zoo animals and even himself into skeletons too. Why does he use this skeleton theme in his battle against Wonder Woman? Would his plans have gone better or worse without all the skeletons?

WRITING PROMPTS

1. Ares turns into a skeleton Chimera to battle Wonder Woman. If you could turn into a mythical creature, what would it be? Write a paragraph describing your creature and draw a picture of it.

2. Wonder Woman stops the skeleton animals from escaping Memorial Park Zoo. But what if she hadn't? Write a short story about the skeleton animals running wild in Gateway City and how Wonder Woman captures them.

3. At the end of the story, Ares ends up trapped in the underworld with Hades. What happens to him next? Write a story about his next plot with his uncle or how he escapes from Tartarus.

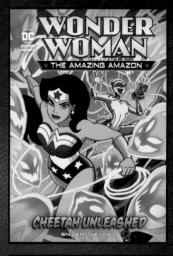